THIN
PLACES

THIN PLACES

LESLEY CHOYCE

DUNDURN
TORONTO

Cover image: Man standing in shaft of light: istockphoto.com/gremlin, Sky: istockphoto.com/Surovtseva
Printer: Webcom

Library and Archives Canada Cataloguing in Publication

Choyce, Lesley, 1951-, author
      Thin places / Lesley Choyce.

Issued in print and electronic formats.
ISBN 978-1-4597-3957-4 (softcover).--ISBN 978-1-4597-3958-1 (PDF).--
ISBN 978-1-4597-3959-8 (EPUB)

      I. Title.

PS8555.H668T45 2017   jC813'.54   C2016-907752-7
                                                C2016-907753-5

1 2 3 4 5   21 20 19 18 17

 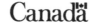

We acknowledge the support of the Canada Council for the Arts, which last year invested $153 million to bring the arts to Canadians throughout the country, and the Ontario Arts Council for our publishing program. We also acknowledge the financial support of the Government of Ontario, through the Ontario Book Publishing Tax Credit and the Ontario Media Development Corporation, and the Government of Canada.

Nous remercions le Conseil des arts du Canada de son soutien. L'an dernier, le Conseil a investi 153 millions de dollars pour mettre de l'art dans la vie des Canadiennes et des Canadiens de tout le pays.

Care has been taken to trace the ownership of copyright material used in this book. The author and the publisher welcome any information enabling them to rectify any references or credits in subsequent editions.

— J. Kirk Howard, President

The publisher is not responsible for websites or their content unless they are owned by the publisher.

Printed and bound in Canada.

VISIT US AT

dundurn.com | @dundurnpress | dundurnpress | dundurnpress

Dundurn
3 Church Street, Suite 500
Toronto, Ontario, Canada
M5E 1M2

INSIDE

When you are young
you have
imaginary friends
right?
         You
make them up and
         hang out with them
have adventures you can
         never have
with real people.
         I had a whole crowd
of friends who
         didn't exist
                  outside of my head.
Real people were
                  well
boring.
Adults were the worst.
They say   How are you?
And I usually say nothing
because I know they can't handle
the truth.

Some ask   What do you want to be
              when you grow up?

And sometimes I answer

> I want to live in my own kingdom
> an island filled with amazing beings
> only I can imagine.

My Imaginary Friends

They
        spoke to me
and told me stories
urged me to do crazy things
        like
make parachutes out of sheets
and jump from
the shed roof.
They suggested I should learn
        to juggle knives
and study the nature of
        fire.
They told me where to look for
ghosts
and demons
and sometimes they
        were not lying
although sometimes
        they just wanted trouble.

(My father said he had a plan
to destroy
my imaginary friends.
That made them very angry.
        But I said
I would never let that happen.)

Mostly
late at night
        they spoke to me
of amazing places
        that could not possibly
                exist.
The voices were always clear
        and
sounded like me.
I guess they were really
        just me
or parts of me.

Let Me Introduce Myself

My parents named me
Declan Lynch
Names are important
> but
it's also important to
> remember
that someone   usually your parents
just made up your name.
You were not born with it.
Think about that.
You
were just   you
when you came into this world.

My mom and dad were the Lynches
living on an average street   Maple Terrace
                                    like the tree
         with the little helicopter seeds.
The Lynches had their first and only kid
me
and said I looked like my great-grandfather
whose name was   Declan Timothy Lynch.
I only saw pictures of my great-grandfather
much later
when I could focus my eyes.

I didn't look anything like him
                but
the name stuck.
Declan
or Deck sometimes
or Declan Patrick Lynch
when I was bad
which was often.
          Just jumping from shed roofs
          getting lost in malls
          hiking deep into the tangled forest
          behind my house
          always determined to not come home on time
          chasing ghosts and demons
          and listening for the next bit of advice
          from the voices in my head.

Parental Advice

My mother told my father
            it was just a phase
I was going through
            a very long phase
and I would grow out
                        of it.
(But she secretly told me
that she understood the voices
and that I should learn the difference
between the good voices
                        and bad ones.)

My father
was a sworn enemy
of my imaginary friends.
            Your imagination
he said
            plays tricks on you
            dirty tricks.
When I asked him what he meant
he tried to explain
but grew frustrated
and stomped away.
I heard him say to my mother in the kitchen
            Sometimes, Fiona

Sometimes I think
that boy is not our son
at all.
Maybe they made a mistake
at the hospital
and gave us
the wrong
child.

OUT OF PLACE, OUT OF TIME

I think I might have been about twelve
>>>> when
one of my imaginary friends
Garth
told me I didn't belong here.
>>>>>>>> Wrong time
>>>>>>>> wrong place
was his way of explaining it.
Garth looked like a cartoon character
except he was real
well, he felt real
and talked real
(with a voice that sounded just like me)
but seemed much wiser than I was.
>>>>>>>> Declan
he told me
>>>>>>>> have you noticed you are different
>>>>>>>> from everyone else?
>>>> Yes
I said.
>>>> But there's not much I can do about it.
>>>>>>>> That's true
he said.
>>>>>>>> But I think someone or something
>>>>>>>> goofed

and you were supposed to be born
a long time ago
or a long time in the future.
Definitely not
here and now.
Which could explain why I never felt like
part of the crowd
like other kids.
Never felt
truly at ease at school
comfortable in groups
or even at home
in my own skin.

Save Me from Myself

Garth's news scared me at first
because I knew
      I would never fit in
and might never
      be happy.
So I started trying to fit in
      to be normal
      have normal conversations
say things like
      Hi, how are you?
and always got predictable answers
so instead I'd ask a kid at school
      What is your favourite planet?
or
      Where were you before you were born?

But
the harder I tried to fit in
the worse it got.
People looked at me
with scrunched-up faces.
The voices in my head got louder
angrier.
Garth said
      You can't deny who you are.

I said

    But I don't know who I am.

And I had an image of myself
unzipping the body I was in

      and travelling someplace else.
A war began inside me
between the me who wanted to be normal
and the me who wanted to leave
and go somewhere else.

One day I screamed it out
in the middle of that tangled forest

    Please!
I shouted.

    Someone save me!

But no one did.
There was only one voice.
The voice was me

    saying I was doomed

      to live in a world

        where I did not belong.

That Was Then

It's a weird thing.
You find yourself
to be sixteen years old
and the voice in your head

                 changes.

It's not your voice
anymore.

       (Where did my voice go?)
       (What the hell is happening to me?)
           It's the voice of

a girl.

           Yes, a girl.

Her voice is beautiful
and she's talking to me.
Yes
talking directly to me.

It went like this:
I was walking home from school
not thinking
about much of anything.
My mind was empty.
Relaxed.
This was a totally new thing

      for me.
I was always agitated
about something.
Now this extremely weird
           calm.

And then
boom. I hear her.
      Declan
she says.

      Declan.
      I'm sorry to
      barge in like this.
It didn't seem like a voice inside.
I was sure it was someone talking.
I looked around but there were only cars and trees
and a cat
but I was sure it was not the cat
talking.
      It will take a while
      to explain myself
she said.
She had a soft and kind voice.
A most wonderful accent
and some kind of funny, beautiful
way of speaking.
      Who are you?
I asked.

Rebecca

she said.

How do you know my name?

Well, I'm inside your head, aren't I?

Are you real?

Yes, very real.

Then let me see you.

Close your eyes.

I closed them.

Can you see me?

Holy shit.

Is that good or bad?

You look like a normal girl.

I'm not really.

Not really what?

Normal, I mean not
normal in the normal sense.

Why?

We should get to know
each other first.

Polite Introductions and Such

I said
            I have to sit down
So I found bench
sat down
and tried to remember
how to breathe.
            I've scared you
she said.   Sorry.
      No.
      I mean yes.
            I knew this would be confusing for you.
      How did you know?
            I know because I know you.
            I've known you for quite a while.
      How can that be?
            It will be hard to explain.
      Try.
            Let me start by saying
            it took a long time to make this connection
            this bridge.
I looked around, my mind reeling.
      What bridge?
            The one between me and you.
            It's how you can hear me
            see me.

None of this was happening out loud.
It was all in my head.
But when I closed my eyes again
I could still see her clearly.

      How do you do this?
         I built the bridge
         to be with you.

      Why me?

And I guess I must have said that out loud because
guys from school were walking by and they
looked at me like I was crazy.

         Weirdo

one said.

         Nutjob

said the other.

Rattled

Yes, rattled.
I wanted the girl
the girl voice
the girl image
to leave me alone
so I could think straight.

         Do you want me to go?
she said.

      No.
      Yes.
      Wait.
      Can you read my thoughts?
         Yes.
      But …
         I know. But it's okay.
         I know *you*.
      But *I* don't know *you*.
         You will.
         If you let me.
And then
she was gone
and the voice in my head
(my own voice)
was just me saying
      What the hell is going on?

Boy Alone on a Park Bench

I've often felt lonely but this was worse.
This was alone alone. Exponentially alone.
And I didn't understand why.
I felt like someone had pulled the plug
that made me me.
I needed to talk to a flesh-and-blood type human being.
So I called Jonesy.

John Jones is his real name but everyone calls him
Jonesy.
He is smart and sad; that's his thing.
He gets an A in every class
even in math and chemistry
but he's never happy with himself or with the world.
You look at him and wonder what he is thinking
why he seems so unhappy.
When he answers his cell phone he just says
                    Ullo.
Just like that.
And it's like he's expecting bad news.
                    Ullo.
          Jonesy, it's me.
                    Deck?
                    What's wrong?
I explained about the voice in my head.

It's really a girl's voice?
Yeah and I can see her too.
What's she look like?
Normal. But kind of hot.
Normal but hot. Hmm.
I think I'm losing it.
I think I've gone over the edge.
I know the feeling.
It passes.
What should I do?
Is she still there
in your head I mean?
No, she thinks she scared me.
So she left.
Where'd she go?
I dunno.
Think she'll come back?
I hope so. I got a lot of questions.
Deck?
What?
You're either mentally ill
or very lucky.

Testing One Two Three

Yes, that's what I heard her saying
in the middle of my dream.

        Is it okay to be here?
she asked   in the middle of a dream.
I had been dreaming about being on a boat that was on fire.

        Then you are just part of my imagination
I said.

        Well yes and no.

        Which is it?

        I have to explain about the bridge first.

        Right, the bridge.

        This is an experiment.

        Being here in your dream.

        What is this? Some kind of science project?

        No. Of course not.

        Declan, you sound angry.

        No. Sorry. It's just that you're freaking me out.

        How'd you get here?

        In my dream.

        It's hard to explain.
I started to feel a little calmer
but then it occurred to me:

        When I dream, I wake up and find out
        the dream is just an illusion.

This is not illusion.

Then let me see you again.

And there she was.

Smiling.

I blurted out

You have really nice eyes

(I'd never seen anything quite like them

large beautiful dark liquid eyes

eyes that could make you forget your own name.)

Thank you

she said. She was smiling.

Can *you* see *me*?

I said.

Of course.

And?

Well, I chose you, didn't I?

What do you mean?

I built the bridge so I could be with you.

Ah, the bridge. Ready to explain?

Not yet.

That's when I woke up.

It was six a.m. according to my clock

and there was sunlight

and the dream was fresh in my head.

I was alone in my room   of course

but now convinced she was not real.

Rude Awakening

Nutjob after all. Not lucky
I concluded.
Time to see a shrink.
Get medicated maybe.
Return to reality.
And then, her voice:

> You don't really want to do that
> do you?

You really can read my thoughts?

> Yes.

I don't know if I like that.

> Sorry.

Why were you in my dream?

> I thought I might be able
> to get closer
> to you.
> I thought
> your barriers might be down.

Right.
But
dreams are kind of messy and confusing.
And private.

But it wasn't just that.
I'd felt invaded

or, what's the word?

Violated.

> Maybe you should stay out of my dreams.

>> Really?

> Really.

>> Okay. Sorry.

Now I could see her again in my head.

> Rebecca

I said out loud.

>> Do you want me to leave you alone?

> No.

The *no* surprised me.

> I want to get to know you
>
> but
>
> I'm gonna need some privacy.

>> I don't understand.

> Well, I
>
> we
>
> um, we all
>
> have a lot of weird thoughts
>
> kicking around in our heads.

>> I've noticed.

>> It doesn't all make sense.

> Can we establish some rules?

>> You mean barriers?

> I mean boundaries.

She looked hurt.

>> How can I explain?

I don't want anyone, even you
reading my every thought
knowing my feelings
being part of my every opinion
listening in on my inner conversations
everything that rattles around in my chaotic
jumble of thoughts.
Watching everything I do.
            Thank you for explaining
she said.
            So how can we make this work?
                        Maybe you can come up with a mechanism
                        a word.
                        You say the word and I leave.
                        You say another word and I come back.
            What can I say when I want some, um, privacy?
I asked.
                        Vega. Say Vega.
            Why that?
                        I don't know. It's the name of a star.
            Okay. When I say Vega, you give me some space?
                        Space. Sure.
I laughed and said
            What happens after Vega, stays in Vega.
                        What?
            Sorry. Stupid joke.
I think she might have laughed
or pretended to laugh.

   Okay then. What if I say
   or think your name
   and you come back?
      Okay
She said.

      Try it. Try the word.
   Vega.
And she was gone without a trace.
   Rebecca?
I said it out loud
feeling some powerful tug inside my chest
just by saying her name.

But she didn't return.

Vega

After she went away
I decided not
to say that word
again
ever.

And Now You Get to Meet My Mom

This required a walk downtown
to her store:
Spiritual Solutions.
The little bell rang when I arrived.
Fiona, my mom, was showing a tray of amethyst crystals
to a customer.
Her face lit up like the sun when she saw me.

                   Declan

she said

                   it's so nice to see you
                   here in the store.
                   It's been a while.

The customer chose a piece of amethyst
handed my mother some money,
smiled, and turned away.
The little bell rang as she left.

My mom and I always had one thing in common:
people considered us a bit strange.
Maybe she's the reason
I am the way I am.
I could tell her things
         I'd never tell my father.

But she always looked worried
when I spoke to her
about
the voices.

But I had to tell someone
other than just Jonesy.
So I told my mom about Rebecca.
Her eyes widened.
                    Do you like her?
she asked.
        I do.
                    Do you know why she is visiting you?
        I don't.
                    Are you keeping an open mind
                    about her?
        I'm trying to.
                    Many great people have heard voices
                    and had visions.
        Many crazy people too.
                    Do you think you are crazy?
        I didn't think so until she appeared.
                    I don't think you are crazy. I think
                    something unique has come your way.
        Well. What should I do?
Despite her words, my mom
suddenly looked terribly anxious.
                    Is she here now?

I closed my eyes and said her name silently.
Nothing.

    No. I may have lost her.

    I told her I needed privacy.

    I'm not sure she understood.

        Be patient.

    What if she doesn't return?

        Then, that is as it was meant to be.

    And what if she does come back?

        Get to know her.

        But Declan

        have you said anything about this

        to your father?

No.

        He's not going to like it.

        Maybe you shouldn't mention it.

Maybe.

        It's just

        well, you know your father.

I nodded, but I'd have to
try to explain it to him
because he'd get furious if he found out
I told my mom and not him.
That had happened before.
Many times.
With bad results.

        And Declan

        about this girl.

Is she cute?

I nodded.

Do you *really*
like her?

I blushed.

Do you trust her?

I think so.
Yeah.
I do.

Then ask her
the most important question of all.

Which is?

Ask her what she carries in her heart.

And that was just like my mom
to say that.
She trusted emotion
and back then I didn't.
But she is
at least partly the reason
I am the way I am.
She had said the right thing
but still
I was a little scared
and confused.
At that moment
I wished I was a little more
like my father

who saw the world
in black and white
and trusted only facts
not belief.

Introducing My Dad

Sometimes you just have to ask
your parents for help.
Even your brainiac father.
My dad, Brendan, was home in his study

reading

a book.

He teaches

physics at the university.
I used to pronounce it "pissicks" when I was little
and it made him laugh.
I wished I could make him laugh
that easily now.

What are you reading?
I asked.

Oh, just a little treatise on a new
twist on
light quantum theory.
The thing looked to be nine hundred pages long.

Is it good?

It makes one think.
Anything that gets the brain going
is good.

Do you mind if I interrupt?

Not at all. This chapter on
monochromatic

radiation can wait.

What if I told you there was this voice
inside my head?

I'd say it's nonsense.

It's your imagination.

Imagination is good

only if it is put to good purpose.

But her voice seems very real.

Her voice?

That's just it. It's a girl's voice.

Hmm. Do you know this girl?

I'm getting to know her.

Is she a girl from school?

No. It's not like that.

Then who is this girl?

She calls herself Rebecca.

Brendan frowned.

Is this

this voice

interfering with your schoolwork?

I lied and said no.

Who is she?

That I don't know. I only know she is in my head.

Can you see her?

Sometimes.

Do you think she is a real person?

I do.

Aside from her voice

and what you see in your head

is there anything, um

tangible about her?

I can't reach out and touch her

if that's what you mean.

Has she told you to do anything crazy?

Like what?

Like jump off a bridge.

It seemed odd that he used that word:

bridge.

I stared at him for a second.

And then he gave me his classic Brendan-the-father

frown.

Declan

he said through clenched teeth

you need to grow up

and stop letting your imagination

trick you like this.

You need to discipline your thoughts.

It was a familiar phrase that often ended

many of our conversations.

And it wasn't the words

as much as the look.

That look always said he was right

and I was being childish.

It was a look that always

always

really pissed me off.

So I refused to say another word
and did what I always did
after a talk like this.
I stomped off to my room
like a little kid.

On the Bus

That's where she returned   on the bus.
I closed my eyes for a brief second
and then I heard her.
   Declan.
  You're back.
   Miss me?
  Sort of.
And then I could see her
inside my head.
I looked around at the other people on the bus.
Some of them were looking at me.
Reading the look on my face.
Probably thought I was on drugs.
So I got off at the next corner.
   Walk with me
I said.
    Can we go someplace private?
  Sure.
And we walked in silence for several blocks
until we came to a path leading into a park
with tall trees and grey squirrels.
   Now what?
    We get to know each other better.
    Ask me anything.
   My mom said I should ask you

what is in your heart?

Wow, you told her about me?

Yes.

And she didn't freak out?

She's not the freak-out type.

But my dad

he did.

You told him too?

Yes.

Her image began to fade.

Wait

I said.

Don't go.

I wasn't going

I just felt …

You felt my worries

my doubts.

I felt

something.

So, what about my question?

I was taking a chance but

I really needed to know

who she was.

Okay

she said.

Here goes.

I came here from a great distance

to find you because

I was very lonely
and I needed to connect to someone.
To you.
That is what is in
my heart.
It took a very long time
to find you.
Why me?
I don't know.
I just knew that if I didn't find you
I would be lost.
Are you supposed to help me in some way?
No.
You
are supposed
to help me.

Upside-Down Universe

That's what it felt like.
Completely wrong.
How could I help anyone
especially her?
I was the one lost
in my own world
a world where I did not belong.
I was looking for a guide
a person with imagination
to help me find a way
to fit in
to survive.
I had convinced myself
Rebecca had come into my head
into my life somehow
to show me the way
to blend
imagination and reality to give me
meaning
and hope.
            Please
she repeated.
            Help me.

Help

That's what she said. I was supposed to help her.
She faded after that
and in her place was an image of

a pile of rocks

on top of a mountain.

I could see the ocean in the distance

and directly below the mountain

green valleys
and other mountains
far away

and I felt wind in my hair.
There was a distinct smell
a distinct smell of

what?

I couldn't nail it down at first
but then I figured it out:

cow shit.

Rebecca
I silently asked.

Why am I smelling cow poop?

CLUES

Then I suddenly lost that image and she was back.

   Did you like it?

  What?

    Where I took you.

    Did you like it?

  Yes, it was interesting

and very beautiful

but a bit smelly.

    That's all you have to say

    about where I come from?

  So that was your home?

    It's near where I live.

    I go up there to reconnect.

  What do you reconnect to?

    You'll need to know me better first

    before I can answer.

  But where was that?

    Guess.

It suddenly occurred to my rattled brain

that Rebecca was an alien.

    Was that the *world* you came from?

      Yes and no.

      I'm still there

      but here.

    At the same time?

Yes.

But before you ask

no, I am not an alien.

Can I take you to another place?

Will it smell like cows?

No. Shut up and close your eyes.

I closed my eyes

I smelled the sea

I smelled the pungent scent of seaweed

and I felt the sea breeze and sun on my face.

I let my mind bring it into focus.

A beach.

A long sand-and-rock

empty beach.

The sea was blue.

There were islands.

Oh my God

I said.

This is my other special place

where I reconnect.

You do a lot of reconnecting.

I need to in order to survive.

It gets lonely

very lonely.

Why?

Not yet

she said.

Not yet.

Research

The voice was gone.
She was gone.
The images
however
were burned into my memory.
I went home
and got online
hoping to track down those images.
I started with beaches.
Do you know how many beaches there are in the world?
A lot. And no one knows the exact number
but some crazy math guy posted what he believes to be
the number of grains of sand in all the world's beaches
which is 5,000 billion billion
or 5 sextillion.
Now you know.
But I digress.
I looked at what seemed like
a thousand
internet images of beaches
but nothing like what I had seen.
All I could figure out from memory
was that it was not a tropical beach
or an arctic beach
or a desert beach

which still left a lot of beaches.
So I gave up on that.

Boy on a Mission

I figured I'd run into the same thing
if I went looking for mountains
so instead, I decided
to look for
piles of rocks.
And
lo and behold
I saw a pile of rocks
like the one I had seen in my head.
A huge pile of rocks
the size of a building
that was man-made
and it had a name.
The pile of rocks
was called a cairn.

Not Just a Pile of Rocks

In ancient times in some parts of the world
people were buried on hilltops or in fields
under a pile of rocks.
Guess it seemed like the thing to do
around 6,000 years ago.
In parts of Europe, the cairns were built with passages
portals to the spiritual world
for the dead.
I saw pictures of them in England
and Scotland and France
and then Ireland.
And then I remembered
an old family photo
of my crazy Uncle Seamus
with my grandfather
standing beside a tall pile of rocks
not like the one in my head
but a pile of rocks nonetheless.

Uncle Seamus Remembered

He was my mother's brother
and he didn't have Skype or internet
or anything like that
but he did have a phone.
I'd been close to him when I was a kid.
Crazy Uncle Seamus, my father called him.
He'd moved here from the west coast of Ireland
to try living in North America
but he didn't like it:

> too crowded
> too fast
> too North American
> bad beer
> everything was metal and
> plastic.

> I likes sea and sky
> and empty fields

he said

> and not much else.

He told me that I should stay in touch
with my Irish heritage.

> You are the only son
> of an only son
> of an only son

   of an only son
   and that
   makes you special.

I didn't really know why
but I got the point.

   Just always remember
   Declan
   It's your adventure
   so you be the hero.

He and my father didn't get along even though my father
had grown up near Seamus in County Sligo, Ireland. My
mother was from there as well, of course. We were an
all-Irish family but my father rejected everything about
the place and swore it was behind him and he — or any
of us — would never go back.

I was sad when Seamus moved back
to his old stone house in Ballyconnell
near the city of Sligo in Ireland.
And then we lost touch
and he just seemed like someone
living in another world.

THE PHONE CALL

I had to look up how to call Ireland
and finally got it right.
Dial 011 and then 353.
It was 10 o'clock at night here
and I wasn't thinking about time zones.

                    Holy Mother of God

he answered.

                    Who would be calling me
                    at two o'clock in the morning?

I didn't know what to say at first.

        It's me

I finally blurted out.

                    Me? Who is me?
                    If you're not the Pope
                    or Saint Patrick himself
                    then I don't want to talk to ya.

        Uncle Seamus, it's me.

                    What?

        Declan.

                    Jesus, boy. Declan.
                    Is something wrong?

        No. Not really.

There was some coughing and throat clearing.

                    Well, then.
                    How are things?

And Then Something Strange Happened

Before I could say anything
I suddenly felt very

           very

                      strange.

I wanted to try to fill in the time
the years
since Uncle Seamus had left.
But I didn't know where to begin.
It was like all my life I was a stranger
living among strangers
an observer watching *me* go through the motions
from a great distance.
           Hello?
Seamus said.
           Declan, you there?
The fog began to clear.
I saw the mountaintop again.
      Sorry
I said.
      It's just that
           Just what?
I didn't know what I had to say
or why I was even calling him
so I reported the only thing

that was now sweeping through my mind.
     I think I'm in love.
          Well then
he said.

          It was worth
          waking up for
          after all.

THE STORY SO FAR

I told Seamus everything:
the voice
the girl
the sea
the beach
the mountaintop
and the pile of rocks — the cairn

      The problem is
I said
      now that she's found me
      I feel less connected to
      anything here.
      Not even my own life.
      I feel like I don't
      belong here.
I took a gulp of air.
      And worse yet
      she's just a voice
      an image in my head.
      I can't be with her
      or touch her.
      I can't …
               Hold your horses
Uncle Seamus said.

       Describe
       that pile of rocks.

So I did.

       Knocknarea

he said suddenly.

       Queen Maeve's tomb.
       You'll need to get over here
       as quickly as you can.
       There's no way around it.

My Parents' Ireland

My mother knew everything
there was to know about her old home
   old Irish beliefs and superstitions
   stones that had magic powers
   Irish saints and the ancient people.
But my father on the other hand
seemed to hate and reject everything
  about the country
  he was born in.
    I grew up in poverty
he said.

   We were held back
   trapped by silly beliefs
   and religion
   and tradition
   and ridiculous stories
   and stupid songs
   and fiddle players
   and drink.
   The only thing that can save Ireland
   is science.
   And maybe even science
   can't save those bloody bumpkins.
And that's what he had to say about Ireland.

MY IRISH BLOOD

My father wouldn't allow books about Ireland in the house
and Uncle Seamus (while he was here)
was an embarrassment
until he abandoned us for the stone house in Ballyconnell
and I couldn't see why being the single son of a single
son, etc.
was important.
And it probably wasn't.
My father said all the single son stuff
about him and me
was "bollocks and shite."
But I wondered sometimes when I was young
what life would have been like for me
if I'd grown up in Ireland.
And now it was in my head again
because *she* was in my head.
And if the cairn made any sense
if Uncle Seamus made any sense
then Rebecca
was Irish
and if she was Irish, I wondered
does that mean she is real?
And if she is real
then …
Then what?

Eight Things Not to Do in Ireland

(Learned from an unreliable source on the internet late at night.)

1. Don't claim to be Irish if you didn't grow up there.
2. Don't fake an Irish accent.
3. Don't ask about leprechauns.
4. Don't ask about "the Troubles."

(I had to look up what the Troubles were and oh boy, they were definitely troubles.)

5. Don't ever try to sing "Danny Boy."
6. Don't kiss the Blarney Stone.

(Locals pee on it at night when the tourists aren't around.)

7. Don't ask for corned beef and cabbage.
8. Don't ask anyone for directions.

(Unless you are prepared to hear their life story.)

One Thing *To* Do in Ireland

Go visit "thin places."
(Learned later that night after falling asleep
and waking up to the voice of Rebecca
in my head.)

Girl in My Bedroom

I had fallen asleep
yes at my computer
and she woke me up.
I was in my underwear
as I heard her voice
and began to see her come into focus
(as the whole room seemed to go out of focus).
      Yikes
I said out loud.
          What?
she said
          You think I've never seen a boy
          in boxer shorts?
I felt my face go red
and scrambled around the room
to find my pants.
      You're from Ireland
I said
      not from some other planet.
          Are you disappointed?
      No. It's just …
          Just what?
      Well, if you are from Ireland
      and you were trying to contact me
      why didn't you just jump on a plane

and come meet me?

I can't do that.

Why?

I'm different

she said it firmly

and didn't explain

so I didn't ask.

Tell me about thin places

I said.

Her face lit up and her eyes widened.

These are places where they say

the spirit world and the physical world

are close together.

Sacred places

ancient burial sites.

Like mountaintops with cairns?

You've been doing your homework.

I told her about my conversation with Uncle Seamus.

You called Ireland?

On the phone. I forgot about time zones.

Time zones are interesting.

If you understand time zones

you'll eventually figure out there are

other kinds of "zones" as well.

Now I'm a little scared.

Don't be.

Hey.

Hey what?

Why don't you tell me your phone number

I said

and I'll call you.

Then we can really talk.

I don't have a phone.

Skype?

No.

Email?

No.

You're a little behind with your technology.

(Maybe I was thinking of my dad's version of Ireland.)

Just the opposite

she said.

I'm way ahead.

You can hear me, right?

See me?

That's true.

Then who needs smartphones or email?

TRAVEL

        I want you to close your eyes

she said.

        I'm going to take you somewhere else.

So I closed my eyes

and suddenly felt like I was falling down a dark endless shaft.

        Don't be scared

Rebecca said.

        That feeling will go away.

And it did.

        Now open your eyes

        but don't really open your eyes.

Strangely, that made sense.

And with my open eyes but eyes still shut

I saw

a little old stone cottage

        Where am I?

        Shush. Just look and listen.

The stone cottage was by a rocky shoreline

on a small cove of some sort.

There was a funny little boat by the shore

and there were fishnets drying on rocks.

The sun was hidden by cloud

and it was drizzling a little

and I heard gulls and lapping waves

and smelled something funny

something burning.
Must have been the smoke from the chimney.

Just then
a man opened the door of the cottage and stepped out
a youngish man smoking a pipe
and he looked up at the sky
as if expecting something.
I noticed then there were no other cottages
no other people
nothing
but grey drippy sky and grey choppy sea
and stone
and then a boy
of about eight
came out of the house
and stood beside the man
who must have been his father.
I waited.
I thought there might be a wife
a mother
but there was no one else.

And then the man turned toward me
as if he knew I was watching.
His eyes were very blue, very intense
and his face
was filled with sadness

as he put his hand
on his son's shoulder.
The boy did not turn toward me
but the man's face
told me a story:
here was the loneliest man
in the world.

LONELINESS SQUARED

When I woke up the next morning
nothing felt right.
Everything seemed wrong:
my thoughts
the room around me
the sky outside my window.
I looked at my hands
like I'd never seen them before.
What was happening to me?
More than ever, I felt
I didn't belong here
only now it was amplified, multiplied
to a point I cannot describe.

I felt like I had somehow been infected
by the loneliness of the man I had seen by the shoreline.
Rebecca had done this to me.
Why?
I had no answers.
The loneliness I now felt
seemed worse because she was not here with me.
Was this some bizarre kind of witchcraft?
Was she a witch?
I didn't believe in witches.
           Rebecca

I silently begged.
        Save me from this
        this feeling.

ENGLISH CLASS

I tried to shake the loneliness
by talking to kids at school
but I wasn't good at it.
I kept saying stupid things
and kids gave me looks
so I gave up
trying to communicate
with them.

Rebecca didn't return until English
in the middle of Mr. Frye reading
from *Julius Caesar* by Shakespeare.
"Men at some time are masters of their fates. The fault,
dear Brutus, is not in our stars, but in ourselves, that we
are underlings."
                    Just keep pretending you are listening
she said.
I nodded.
Rebecca knew that when she appeared
when we were in conversation
I "acted weird"
not exactly speaking out loud
but distracted.
After all, I was seeing someone
that no one else could see.

But just then, Mr. Frye was looking at me.
He'd seen me nod.

        Do you agree then, Declan?
Frye asked.
I must have looked puzzled.
It was a look I often had.

        Are we masters of our own fate?
       Tell him that not everyone is.
       Tell him you have to choose to be master
       of your own fate.
I repeated her words verbatim.
Now Mr. Frye nodded, smiled, and continued to read.

Rebecca stayed "with me"
(I knew she was still there)
but remained silent until the end of class.
I went to the library and sat way in the back
at a computer.

       Why did you show me that man and his son?
I asked.

       Because you needed to see them.
       You needed to see the look on his face.
     I didn't just see it
I said.

     I felt it.

       I know you did.
       I needed you to feel his loneliness.
   Why?

Declan, there's so much to explain.

Then explain, please.

I kept expecting her image to appear in my mind as before.

But I could not see her.

And her voice was faint

like someone had turned down the volume

on a television.

Declan, soon I won't be able to visit you.

It requires too much energy.

I need you to come here.

How?

Fly, Declan.

Come soon.

Please.

Help me, Jonesy

Jonesy had been looking for me
all over the school.

>> Declan

he said

>> you look like
>> you've seen
>> a ghost.

> Help me, Jonesy

I said

> I'm in over my head.

>> Mental illness is like that.
>> How can I help?

I explained about what happened in English class.
He said

>> I wish my English classes
>> were that interesting.

> She wants me to meet her.
> To go to her.

>> Do you have to leave the planet
>> and leave your body behind?

Jonesy was serious, the goof.

> No.
> It's not like that.

>> Where then?
>> Where do you need to go?

I've got images in my head
of where I'm supposed to go.
Ireland.

Ireland?

Jonesy asked
as a big smile came over his face.

She's Irish.
You're Irish too
deep down in your
inner self.

What should I do?

I asked.

I'm kinda scared.

And I was.
I was so far deep into something
way over my head.

Scared is good.
But not enough.

What then?
What else?

You need to be brave.

Flying to Knocknarea

No, Rebecca did not mean "fly"
like jump off roofs
or grow wings
or leave my body
or anything more far-fetched.
She meant get on a plane and fly there to meet her.
She never told me *where* or even exactly *how* to meet her.
But I'd seen those images.
Knocknarea — a mountain
and the beach
and the cove
and what did that man and his son
have to do with anything?
I didn't know what to make
of the fact I could not see her now
and that her once crystal clear voice
was fading.
But what scared me even more was this.
What if I lost her altogether?
I couldn't bear that.

Report Card

My father was furious.
My grades which had never been good
were slipping
because I was being distracted by Rebecca
falling in love with her
and wishing I was with her.
She was on my mind constantly now.

One night my mother asked me about "the girl"
and I was evasive.
Not that she wouldn't take me seriously.
It was just that she might share
what I said with my father.

      I think I might need to leave school for a while
I told her.

                 Why?

      I just need to.
      I need to go someplace different.
      I want to go stay with Uncle Seamus.

                 In Ireland?

      Yes.
When she said the word, it was like an awakening.
I heard Rebecca loud and clear then.
Only two words.

           Yes!
           Please!

Parental Battleground

My mother made the case to my father
about sending me to stay with Seamus
until the school year was over.
I could make up the work in the summer
she said. In summer school.
She told him I was under too much stress.
I was alienated from the other kids.
I needed a break
for my mental health.

My father hated the idea.
He ranted and raved about how Ireland would be bad for me
how Seamus was a lunatic and a lazy bastard.
Then an argument began
unlike any I'd heard from them in my life.

My father: Jesus, Fiona, the boy needs to grow up. He
needs to be responsible for his actions. He needs to think
straight and get his life together. You've put foolish notions
in his head ever since he was a boy. Now this!

My mother: Yes, Brendan. Now this. He's unsettled, yes.
He is not a great scholar like yourself. He is old enough
now to find his place in the world. And that place is not
here. We must help him.

My father: What? By sending him to live with Seamus, a man who can't tie his own shoes much less hold down a job? A man who whines for the days gone by in a mythical Ireland that never existed? We left that damp, dingy rock to make a life here. A life for us and a life for our son. The answer is final. He is not going.

My mother said nothing more.
I heard her stomp off to the bedroom and slam the door.
I felt the guilt of a son
who had driven a wedge between
two loving people who
did not deserve the grief
caused by a lovestruck and bewildered son.

A Turn of Events

But then something happened.
At school.
The following week.
A kid with a gun.
A loaded gun.
He walked into a classroom
and held the gun
to a teacher's head.
The school went into lockdown.
I was in the library at the time.
The librarian, Mrs. Kendish
locked the doors and told those of us in the room
to get down on the floor.
I had been near the windows looking at books
on mythology.
Kneeling on the floor, I heard Rebecca's voice

        Declan

        Don't be scared.

I wanted to tell her that I wasn't scared
but then I realized her brief presence had suddenly vanished
and I saw the face of that man again.

The good news is that no one got shot.
The police came, and someone talked the kid
out of hurting anyone.

I didn't know him.
He was new.
He had that lost look
the one people said I have sometimes
the look I'd seen on Jonesy.
But I saw something else as well
some kind
of pain I couldn't imagine.

So our school was in the national news
and I thought it would all
just go away after the incident
since no one got hurt.
But it didn't.
Everything about school was different.
Kids were nervous.
Teachers were nervous.
Some parents pulled their kids from school.
My mom asked me if I felt safe there.
I lied.
I said no.
I said I was scared.
That I couldn't quite get back to normal.

                                  Okay

she said

                            I'm going to talk this over
                            with your father.

A Theory for Everything

My father the physicist had a theory for everything.
Why the economy is not good.
Why atoms behave the way they do.
Why the universe came into existence.
Why we don't get sucked into black holes.
Why starlings gather in flocks in the yard.
Why some kids take guns and walk into schools.

And he had a theory about me:
one day a light bulb
would turn on in my head
and I'd start taking charge of my life.
My true ability to reason
and make rational decisions would kick in.
I would show some effort at school
and become
really
really
engaged.
That was his word: engaged.

But the school thing scared my mom
and my mom
in turn
scared him.

He became
convinced
there was a real chance that his son
might get shot.

One crazy kid with a gun

he said

inspires a second crazy kid
with a gun
and next time
that kid is going to shoot.

It was just a theory.

BUT

But, it was *his* theory
and my mom bought into it
and I pretended that I bought into it.
   I want to go somewhere safe
I said.

   Somewhere where there are
   not so many guns about.
   Ireland
I said.

   Ireland *is* the light bulb in my head.
   But it's more like a spotlight
I told him
   shining through all the darkness.
I did not mention Rebecca
or that I was in love with her
(whoever, whatever she was).

     Why Ireland?
he insisted.

     Why can't it be any place
     other than Ireland?
   Uncle Seamus
I said.

   He invited me to stay with him.
     Your Uncle Seamus

is a lunatic
a true pureblood
Irish lunatic.
I don't care if he is
your mother's brother.
He's a menace.
My mom gave my dad a dirty look.
Do you have a second choice?
I thought for a few seconds.
Egypt
I said.
I'll go to Egypt.
My dad looked at me.
He'd been watching the news.
Egypt was going through some nasty violent times.
His eyes were wide.
He looked flustered.
He had a dozen or so theories about the Middle East.
None of them were pretty.

He stared at his son
his more than slightly off-kilter son
his son who could end up brainwashed
by his lunatic brother-in-law.
There was confusion in his eyes
that I don't believe I had ever seen
before.
And I guess Ireland ultimately

beat out Egypt
in some crazy emotional football game
going on
in his head.

MY FATHER'S LIST OF THINGS TO DO AND NOT TO DO IN IRELAND

I read it on the plane to Shannon.
It went like this:

1. Don't hang out in pubs.
2. Don't believe anything an Irishman tells you.
(They're unbelievable liars.)
3. If anyone asks you your religion, say you are a
Buddhist.
4. Don't tell anyone you have Irish blood.
5. Convince your Uncle Seamus to get a real job.
(Playing a fiddle is not and never will be real work.)
6. Don't allow yourself to get beguiled by an Irish girl.
(They can trick you, fool you, and who knows what.)

Well, my dad had, I guess, become "beguiled" by my mother.
Two more opposite personalities could not exist on the
planet. My dad considered himself "a hard-nosed realist."
My mom kept amethyst crystals under her pillow. She also
gave me a piece of "sacred" Irish jade for good luck to carry
with me at all times.

33,000 FEET

It was a bumpy ride across the Atlantic at 33,000 feet
and I was pretty sure it was the jade
that kept the plane in the air
until the green green shores of Ireland
appeared in the airplane window
and beckoned the plane to land
safely in Shannon
where the immigration man
looked at the picture of me
on my passport
and then at me
and smiled in a funny way
like he knew something
I didn't.

LIKE COMING HOME

That's what it felt like.
Coming home.
Like I'd been here before.
Like I was *meant* to be here.
Like I was (pardon the word)
destined
to be here.
I was a boy just off the plane
on my own
in Ireland.
And I felt like anything
anything
could happen.

All I needed to do
was
find
her.

THE BUS

I took the bus
north through towns with crazy names:
Ennis, Gort, Galway, Tuam, Knock
Tobercurry, Knockbeg, Colooney
and then the city of Sligo.

THE LONG WAY HOME

Uncle Seamus met me at the bus station in Sligo.
He'd had a few pints and had been playing fiddle
in a nearby pub.
He asked me to drive us home
and reluctantly I did.
I'd only driven a few times,
and the steering wheel was on the
wrong side of the car.
As I drove
poorly and cautiously
he told tales of his youth
some true
some probably not.
I tried my best to stay on
the left-hand side of the narrow roads.

                 That clutch

said Seamus

                    is quirky as a pheasant in heat.

White knuckles on my part
turning on to
Drumcliff at the base of a mountain
Benbulben
then west to Carney
Cloghboley
and finally

Ballyconnell

              Bally Bliss
              I calls it
my uncle said.
And suddenly
there we were
way out at the westerly edge of Ireland
at what seemed to be
the end of the earth.

First Night in Ireland

It was a cold stone house
with wind whistling in the eaves
and a peat fire
that smelled so good
it put me to sleep
by nine o'clock.
Not a word or an image
from Rebecca
and I wondered if I had made a mistake.
Connected the dots the wrong way.
Maybe I should have gone to Egypt.
Seamus' words were still in my head:

> In the morning
> we climb Knocknarea
> and pay our respects
> to Queen Maeve.

WARRIOR QUEEN

Queen Maeve

Seamus told me

was an ancient warrior queen
or goddess perhaps
who was very rich
and powerfully sexual
and one day she stole
an enormous and strong bull
from Ulster
for reasons that may elude us today.
She was not exactly well liked
by her subjects and perhaps
they buried her on the remote
mountaintop of Knocknarea
where her spirit could
do no harm.

I tried to envision this queen
hoping that Rebecca would read my thoughts
and comment
telling me
that women in Ireland rarely
steal bulls
anymore.

But instead, I only heard the wind.

KNOCKNAREA

The drive to Knocknarea was through
an enchanted land:
green fields
and stone walls
sheep and cows
and old men sitting on benches
looking like they were from another century
and didn't give a damn about this one.

I drove with difficulty and shaky hands
and Seamus talked.

Finally as we pulled into
the small parking lot at the base of Knocknarea,
I interrupted him
     How do I find the girl?
I asked.
     How do I find Rebecca?
          Maybe you don't
he said, smiling.

          Maybe she'll find you
          if she's ready.

The trail was steep and full of rocks.
Seamus sang
     In the merry month of May

> *from me home I started*
> *Left the girls of Tuam*
> *nearly broken-hearted*
> *Saluted father dear,*
> *kissed me darling mother*
> *Drank a pint of beer,*
> *me grief and tears to smother*

and so on.

A little way along I caught the smell of cow shit
as earthy as I had imagined it.
At that moment nothing could have smelled sweeter.

The top was blustery and cold
and before us was that giant pile of rocks
each stone placed where it should be by human hands
from Neolithic times.
The cairn was a monument and a grave
and considered by some to be sacred.
The view was magnificent
just as I had seen in the vision
that Rebecca put in my head.

      Is this one of the thin places?
I asked as I stared at the stones
and let the wind whip my hair into a frenzy.

              Don't get much thinner
              than this

Seamus reported.

And I expected any minute for Rebecca
the flesh and blood Rebecca
to walk from behind the cairn
and take my hand.

But she did not.
Instead
clouds slowly shifted in from the west
and the wind increased
and pelting cold rain
fell from the heavens.
We turned
and clambered down
the sides of Knocknarea
breathing hard
and fast
as we hurried
and stumbled
on the never-ending stones
once walked upon
by the ancients.

AFTER KNOCKNAREA

On the subject of women Seamus was surprisingly mute.
I was a smitten teenage boy
in love (or at least believing he was in love)
with the girl of his
dreams.
Literally   come to think of it.
Days passed after Knocknarea
and she did not appear.
                         Ireland is a big place
Seamus reminded me.
                    She could be in Donegal or County
                    Clare
                    or Tipperary or Cork.
He suggested I was in trouble though
if she were to be living in Dublin
but he wouldn't explain why
except to say he didn't trust that dirty city
or anyone in it.

I asked him why he lived alone
and why he had not married.
This brought a faraway look to his eyes
and at first I thought he wouldn't say a word.
But then the floodgates opened.

Seamus Speaks

I was a mere country lad meself
and had not a care in the world
except to work on McGonnigle's farm
mucking around with the cows and such
and meeting up with me mates for a pint at the pub.
And then I met Katherine.
Long dark hair and fair of skin
and eyes that would look into your very soul.
Her father hated me
as fathers do when a young man
captures a daughter's heart
and I tried to convince him of my worth
which was an utter failure on my part.
She was Catholic and I was Protestant
but if you had asked me to choose between
God and the girl I loved
it would have been no contest at all.
Still
these things
these differences
run deep in this country.

Katherine had ambition and wanted to go
to university.
A rare thing for a girl from these parts

in those days.
But I was all for that
and would follow her to the ends of the earth
even to Dublin if need be.

And then she got pregnant
and she did not tell me.
I knew something had changed
but had no idea
what must have been
going through her mind.
She went somewhere
to Limerick I think
and had the pregnancy terminated.
Abortion was not legal, of course
and had she told me
I would have convinced her to keep the baby.
We
would have kept the baby.
But she didn't.
Afterward
when she came home
there was an infection.
She died.
And a big part of me
died with her.

Her father tried to kill me.
Once with a peat spade
and once with an axe
and he would have satisfied us both
had he succeeded
but in the end he couldn't do it
and we both fell to this very floor beneath you
Declan
weeping
until the neighbours came.
And after that
well
after that
here you see me.
There's not much more to say.

Paths to Nowhere

After a few uneventful days
Uncle Seamus said I should take the car
any time I wanted.
My driving by now
had improved.
I studied the road maps and found
my way to other ancient places:
Carrowmore
and Carrowkeel
with more piles of rocks and dolmans
(stone tombs said to have passages to other worlds)
but not a sign of Rebecca.

Like Uncle Seamus
I felt   like   I had lost
the love
of my life.

On my way home one day
I stopped at the old church in the town of Drumcliff
and found the grave of the Irish poet
W.B. Yeats
with its inscription:

> "Cast a cold Eye
> On Life, on Death,

Horseman, pass by."

Towering above the graveyard
was the mountain
called Benbulben.
I drove down a potholed single-track road around its base
and hiked up into fields and forest paths
                to find a way
                to the summit
                buried in the clouds.
Surely, there I would hear her voice
                or see her in my
                mind's eye.
But I failed to find a path
                allowing me a way up.
And then
                all alone in an empty
                pasture
a dark cloud descended
the very sky
                dropping down on me
like nothing I'd ever known
and again I felt terribly alone
and abandoned.
                Something had gone out
                of the world.
Not just the sun
not just my old familiar life

but now
I was losing hope I'd ever see Rebecca again.
                       I felt hollow
                       and weak
                       and lost
as that great malignant cloud
first swallowed the top of Benbulben
then settled on the field
and swallowed me
in midday darkness.

Saved by a Horse

I sat there on a great cold stone

            and thought I
            would cry.

At my feet I noticed
a small mound of sand
as if something created
by ants.
But the sand itself puzzled me.
When I looked up

            there was a horse.

A pony, really.
I would learn later   it was
a Connemara   pony.
It appeared coming through the mist
walking my way.
A pale grey-white creature with magnificent eyes
walking straight to me   as if
I had called out to it.
I reached out   and was permitted to touch
her head   stroke her back.
I imagined there was something spiritual
about this beautiful creature
who stood there beside me
as if protecting me   from something unknown

or from myself   perhaps.
But I still sank deeper into my gloom
until the horse bowed its head

                         and nudged my side
almost knocking me off my stone perch.
For unknown reasons

                         I bent over
                         and scooped some sand
                         (no ants)
                         and dumped it in my
                         pocket.
Then   I began to walk
down toward where I had parked the car.
The horse followed me to a fence
and before I climbed over
I saw that there was a single ancient
standing stone behind me in the field
a monument to what, I didn't know.
The horse watched as I placed
my hands
on the stone
half expecting some message to come to me
from another time.
And then I heard a voice

                         a whisper really.
I looked around

                         but saw nothing.
Then I heard it again:

Keep looking

she said.

I need you
to find me.

THE LONELY MAN

He appeared to me again in my sleep
                              standing by his stone
                              hut.
His eyes pierced me and frightened me.
                              I woke up
                              shaking.
I must have screamed as well
because Seamus came into my room
and turned on the light.
                    Lad?
He asked.
                         Are you all right?
          It was just a dream
I said.
                    Perhaps
he said.
                    This girl who's haunting you
                    perhaps
                    she's a witch
                    and she is trying
                    to do you harm.
And then he told me about the eight witches
of Islandmagee
on trial in 1711.

Hauntings

On the peninsula of Islandmagee
in County Antrim
a widow awoke one night and found
her sheets and blankets ripped off
and folded into the shape of a corpse.
Rocks were thrown at her windows
and she heard voices telling her
she would die.

And die she did
in awful pain.

Later, the woman's knotted apron was found
by a beautiful eighteen-year-old girl
named Mary
who untied the knots.
Immediately after
she began to see demon horses in the clouds
and saw a nightgown walking by itself.

Mary had become possessed
and vomited pins and buttons
shouted and screamed hysterically
and was seen floating above her bed.

Eight women in the village
were charged with being witches.
They were later convicted
and thrown into filthy dungeons
in Carrickfergus.

But they survived.
The people of Islandmagee
were convinced they
were witches
but not the only ones
causing mayhem.

BELIEF

No
I told Seamus.

I don't believe in witches.

But you're in Ireland, now
he said.

You already told me you came here
looking for the special places
where the spirit world is closer
to the physical world.

But it's not like that
I insisted.

There is nothing evil about Rebecca.
He gave me a funny smile
as
he so often did and said

Well, we're all glad of that.

And I told him about what woke me
not Rebecca
but the man.

Describe where he lived.
So I described the stone hut
and the boat.

It's called a *currach*

Seamus said

a boat made from a wooden frame

with animal skins stretched over it.
It can be rowed by one or more men
out to sea for fishing.
And then he added for emphasis
Your friend
he's a fisherman.
He lives by the sea.
I was staring at the floor now
and noticed the sand
a small sprinkling of it
on the worn floorboards
that must have spilled from
my jacket pocket.

BEACHES

Seamus wrote me a list
of all the beaches he knew of
in County Sligo and beyond.

He offered to join me in my search
and seemed rather disappointed
when I said I needed
to go at it alone.

I drove first south to Strandhill

                    with its dunes

true mountains of sand.

                     I trudged to the tops

and back down to the stony beach
but grand as it was
I saw no fisherman's hut
felt no presence of spirit.
Before I left the town
I stopped in a little shop
called Shells
run by surfers
where I bought a piece of amethyst
for my mother.
It made me feel homesick

               for the first time.

I missed her

            and my father as well

and began to doubt

            why I was here.

As I walked back toward the shore

I heard my father's clear voice of reason

            saying

there was nothing here to find.

I had followed a foolish notion

            to a foreign shore

where I didn't belong.

The Coasts of Sligo

But later that day
my father's cold logic faded
as I passed green fields
and sunlit lakes.
I was getting good with the driving
and following
the map Seamus had given me
marked with the coves and beaches:
Rossnowlagh, Mullaghmore
Raghly, Moneygold.
Some of the beaches were in towns
and some were tourist destinations
and nothing felt right
but I walked them all
inch by inch
waiting for her voice
waiting for something.

CALL FROM HOME

It was my father.

> Your mother told me why
>
> you are really in Ireland

he said

his voice filled with anger.

> You are to come home at once.

> I would
>
> if I could

I said.

> But I can't.

> Put on your Uncle Seamus.

So I handed Seamus the phone.

I could hear my father shouting at him:

> Seamus, you old fool
>
> do one sensible thing in your life
>
> and put my boy on a feckin' plane.
>
> Send him back home.

And I could see Seamus getting angry himself

but he held the phone away from his ear

and said nothing in return.

When my father's rage subsided

Seamus simply said

> Brendan
>
> your son
>
> needs to see this through.

And then he took a breath
and added

        no matter how foolish.

Down and Out in Ballyconnell

Two more days of scouring the coast
and nothing to show for it
but a sunburnt nose
and diminished spirit.
So I decided to enter
my first Irish public house:
The Yeats Tavern
named after the poet
in Drumcliff.
The man behind the bar looked me over
when I asked for a pint of Guinness
and was about to turn me down
when a young man of about twenty
sat down beside me.
He looked sunburnt too and tired
and gave me a curious look.

                    Tom
he said to the bartender

                    Give this gentleman his pint.
                    It's on me.
I thanked him and watched the ritual
of the slow and steady
pouring of the dark beer.

          Thanks
I said to both Tom and the sunburnt guy.

You looked like you needed it

he said.

I'm Alfie.

He held out his hand.

Declan

I said, shaking it.

Declan, I detect in you unhappiness.

He had that Irish way

of pronouncing every syllable with precision.

I took my first sip of Guinness

and I think I frowned.

It was bitter.

I don't know what I was expecting.

You detected correctly

I said

and this made Alfie laugh.

He ordered himself a Smithwick's.

From away then?

he asked.

Yes.

What brings ya?

At first I didn't know what to say

knowing it would sound silly.

A quest

I said finally.

Ah, yes.

The plot thickens.

Is it fame, fortune, or salvation?

Not really.

Then it must be a woman

he asserted.

I didn't want to go there so I said

I'm looking for a beach

and he laughed.

Lots of beaches about.

This one is special.

Every beach is special.

Alfie explained that he was a surfer

and he had given up working for Google in Dublin.

I moved west, here to the coast

and never looked back.

I said

I've been to every beach around

but I haven't found the right one

the one I've seen in a vision.

A vision quest, is it?

Name the beaches you've been to.

So I pulled the road map out of my back pocket

and pointed to them one by one.

Alfie studied the map

and then pointed to a spot.

You missed one

he said.

Streedagh.

I was there this morning.

Waves head high and glassy

and not a soul around.

Some of the best waves I ever surfed.

I wanted to ask more but was afraid

I'd discover yet another dead end.

And then Alfie finished his Smithwick's

in three long gulps

shook my hand and was off.

Let me know if you find

what you're looking for.

End of the rainbow and all that.

Streedagh

There were horses grazing in open pasture land
by the dunes.
They looked like they had been expecting me.
I got out of the car
and breathed in the cool salty air.
There was a cluster of houses at one end
but beyond that
the beach stretched out
for what looked like several empty miles.
I put on a jacket and began walking.

The Sand, the Sea, the Sky

At first it seemed

        that it was just

                another beach.

But as I walked

        I felt

             something.

A presence.

        Three times

I stopped and turned around

        expecting some   thing

           some   one

to be there.

But it was all in my imagination.

I was a guy alone on a beach

with an addled brain

walking to nowhere.

THE COVE

I had almost decided
to turn back
when I came to a small
rocky cove.
In the dunes
was the ruins of
an old
stone building.
I angled toward it
and touched a thick lichen-covered stone wall
or what was left of it
now only shoulder high.
A cottage
           someone's small
           primitive hut really
           long, long since
           abandoned.
I knelt down
              expecting maybe
              to find some relic
              some scrap or tool
but nothing.

And then as I stood up
and turned around

looking out onto the cove
and beyond to the mountains
and a distant shore
        I recognized the view.
This had once been
the home
        of that sad lonely soul
        that fisherman
        and his little boy.

Night

Each time I tried to leave the spot
something tugged me back.
                        I had this feeling
that if I left
                I could never return.
Or if I did return
                        the ruins would be gone.
So I sat in the chill salt air
                huddled by the stone wall
my knees to my chest.
                        I watched
as the sun set over the sea
                and the stars came out
a canopy of a million points of light.
I felt giddy at first
        in expectation of what I didn't know.
Giddy, then a little fearful.
                        Wild creatures were about.
I could hear them
        but I couldn't see them.
And then
cold
and bored
and tired
I fell asleep.

And while I slept
I felt a new wave of overwhelming sadness
a paralyzing sense of loneliness
beyond what I had known before.
It felt like some kind of heavy weight
pressing down on me
and it would not go away
until I felt
the warmth
of the morning sun
on my face.

Morning

She was the first thing I saw
when I opened my eyes
sitting directly in front of me.
                You found me
she said.
                I was afraid you wouldn't.
Her arms were wrapped around her knees.
        So was I
I said.
                I knew you were here
                in Ireland
                and I wanted so much
                to come to you
                but I couldn't.
                I needed to stay close
                to here.
        Why?
                Soon
she said.
                I'll explain soon.
I leaned forward and inched across the sand and stone
on my hands and knees
and then
I touched her face.
                Checking to see if I'm real?

I felt her cheek with my fingers
touched her brow
and then ran my fingers through
her long dark hair
as she closed her dark eyes
and reached out to touch my face.
And then she leaned forward
and kissed me.

I sat upright and then pulled her toward me.
She seemed to melt into my arms
into me
as we lay on the ground inside the ruins of that house
alone in our perfect little world
where language seemed obsolete.

Rebecca

> This place?

I asked.

> Why here?
>> This is my home
>> my history.
>> I came ashore
>> there.

She pointed to the cove
the water sparkling in the morning sunlight
with perfectly sculpted waves rolling shoreward.

> Where did you come from?

She pointed again to the sea.

> These ruins

I said.

>> This was the stone hut
>> where that man stood
>> with his son?

She nodded.

> You planted that image in my head, right?

She nodded again.

> Why?
>> So you'd find me.

THE PAST

Part of me wanted to stop asking questions.
I had found her.
We were together.
What else mattered?
But my mind was filled with the need to know more
to know everything.

I went to the mountain

I said.

Knocknarea

just like you showed me.

Why didn't you meet me there?

I couldn't.

I needed to stay here.

Who was the man I saw in the dream?

He was my husband.

Your husband?
A wave like some kind of
cruel electric shock
passed through my brain.
This made no sense.
I couldn't believe what she had just told me.

And the boy?

He's your son?

No. Not mine. *His.*

I don't understand.

That was all a very long time ago.

I still don't understand.

How long?

    Three hundred years.

TIME

Are you some kind of time traveller?
I asked.

   We all travel through time, Declan.
   But no. Not like that.

Does this have something to do
with the bridge you told me about?

   It was the connection I made
   with you.
   You were the one
   I was waiting for.

Why me?

   It's what I sensed in you
   what I felt.
   You were somehow
   not of this time.
   And you were searching for something.

What was I searching for?

   You didn't know what it was.

And then I found
you.

There were several seconds of silence
and then she smiled and said

   The truth is
   I found *you*.

But how can you …

How can I be so old?

She looked to be sixteen, maybe seventeen.

I nodded.

Time is a strange thing, Declan.

I'll try to explain.

Rebecca's Tale

I came from the sea.
I was not the first.
There were many like me.
The man I introduced you to in your dream
was Liam
a fisherman
whom I had seen at sea many times.
He was a good man
a kind man
and then his wife died.
I felt his pain
so intensely
that I chose to come ashore
to change my form.
He needed me.
His son needed me.

BELIEF

This was three hundred years ago?
I asked.

Yes.
And you were
not human?

I became human
when
I felt the tug
an overwhelming need
to save this man and his son
from their loneliness and pain.
In my world
the world I came from
such things are possible.
What were you before you became human?
You will not understand if I tell you.
I don't understand any of this
but I do know I am here with you now
and don't want to lose you.
And I do want to understand.

I was a *roane*
she said in that beautiful odd way of hers
a *selchidh*.
I lived in the *Domnu*
the deep ocean

with my kind.
I was a seal.
When we go through the change
and come ashore
they call us selkies.

LIAM

She told me of Liam
truly a good man if ever there was one
and how he accepted her as a gift from the sea
how she adapted to his rough life ashore
and helped raise his son, Fergus.
But Liam grew older
and Rebecca did not.
Liam accepted this and loved her with all his heart
but
as Fergus got older
he grew to fear her
and thought she was a witch.
Fergus moved away when he was twenty-one
and never spoke to his father
again.

        I watched as Liam aged

Rebecca said

        and the sadness grew within me.
        I watched as he suffered
        from the hard work of hauling nets
        and dragging his *currach* ashore.
        I loved him very much
        and the pain I felt as he grew old and sick
        was the price I paid for saving him from
        his loneliness.

LIFE AT STREEDAGH

They had lived very much alone at Streedagh
and Rebecca was happy to live close to the shore
by the sea where she had come from.
If anyone passed by
they would just see a figure in an old woman's clothing
bent over or with her face covered.
Few cared about Liam after his son moved on
and if anyone spoke of "his woman"
they would say she was crazy
and all were glad
she kept to herself
out of the way of society.
When Liam died
she buried him in the dunes.
One day
Fergus returned
and blamed Rebecca for Liam's death.
He saw that still she had not aged
and he spit on her
then left
and began spreading the rumours
that she was a witch.

Rebecca Speaks

I had to leave.
I had no choice.
I could not go back to the sea
even though
I longed for the comfort of the deep.
But I was in human form
and could not change back
until I found someone with whom
I could create
a strong enough emotional bond
to save me from what I'd become.
A wandering lost soul
hiding from the world
a world
where I did not belong.

I searched for a very long time.
With my thoughts
I spoke to some who
I thought could help.
But none could.
And then you came to me.
I saw you first in a dream.
And then I found you
and spoke to you.

I believed that creating the bridge
to you
would ultimately
bring you here
and our bond
would give me back the strength
I needed
and therefore the ability
to return
to my true home.

What I Know

Stop talking
I said.
Just stop the story.
Sorry
I meant to give you
a little at a time.
I held her at arm's length now
one hand on each shoulder.
All I know
all I care about
is that I have found you
and we are together.
She smiled then
the smile I had seen in my visions of her
the girl who was the voice in my head.
The girl who had visited me
on the other side of the ocean
was now real flesh and blood
here and now.
Can you love me
the way you loved Liam?
Yes.
What if we rebuild a house
right here?
That would be wonderful.

WORDS

Even as I heard myself speak the words
I began to believe I had slipped over into
some new kind of fantasy world.
None of this could be real.
The voice in my head perhaps
was the first sign of delusional behaviour
and now I'd taken it too far.

       Let's walk

I said.

       You need to tell me what
       you've been doing
       for the last three hundred years.

She explained that she had to keep moving
from town to town
so people did not notice that she did not age.

       Friends I made
       for short spells
       but no lovers.
       People stopped believing in witches
       and that helped.
       But I could not bear
       to watch people get sick
       get old
       die.

Do you mean that you can live
forever?

No.

We all have a limited life force.

I think it was the way she said those words
like a line from one of those science fiction movies
I used to like.

It became convincingly clear
that Rebecca was a product of my imagination
my dementia
or whatever had happened to me.

She stopped and looked at me.

There was something else in her look now.

Something that scared me.

In her

I now saw

anger.

You don't believe me

she said.

You don't believe I am real.

And then she suddenly began
walking away from me.

She looked around on the sand as she walked.

I ran to catch up
just as she found
a shard of glass
the neck of a broken bottle.

I did not move quickly enough

to stop her from jabbing it into her arm
wounding herself.
I grabbed the piece of glass and threw it into the sea
and pressed my hand against her wound.
As I held my hand there
I couldn't believe that I had just doubted her.

       I'm real

       dammit.

       This is real.

As I pressed harder on the wound
the blood continued to spill and drip on the white sand.

       I'm sorry

I said
and walked her to the shoreline
where I cupped salt water to pour on her arm.
It stopped bleeding quickly.
The wound was not deep
but something about pouring sea water on it
made her react.
Her eyes grew suddenly wide.

       Please don't leave me

she said.

       I won't leave you

I said.

       Ever.

Uncle Seamus

I told her about my uncle and that he would be
worried about me.
Could she go with me to meet him?
She shook her head no.
      Please
I begged.
      It's important.
         Okay.
         But I can't stay away
         from here for long.
         I need to be here.
I didn't ask any further questions.

I walked in alone at first.
Seamus was blustering and angry
wanting to know where I'd been
since the day before
what I'd been up to with his car.
      Fell asleep at the beach
I said
      I'm sorry.
      But I met a girl.
         A girl?
he asked.
         The girl.

Holy Mother of God

Seamus said.

Would you like to meet her?

Seamus didn't say a word.

He blinked and just stared at me.

I took that as a yes.

Introductions

Rebecca looked shy and tired
as she entered the house.
Seamus tried to say something
but   instead
he just   stared at her.
I fumbled my way through introductions
but I don't think he was listening.
                    I know you
Uncle Seamus suddenly said.
                    I know you from somewhere.
          I don't think so
Rebecca said
sounding sheepish and a bit fearful.
Seamus looked more closely at her.
                    Oh
                    maybe not
he said.
                    I'm getting old
                    and memory does funny things.
Then he took a deep breath
 offered us some tea and we all sat down
in a pool of sunlight
at the kitchen table.
Rebecca now looked drained of energy.
Seamus, his back to us

babbled a bit of his usual blarney
about nothing in particular.
I was growing worried about Rebecca.
I needed to take her back to Streedagh.

Sorry, Uncle Seamus

I think we need to leave
I blurted.
That's when he dropped the china teapot
and it shattered on the stone floor.

Holy Mother of God

Seamus said again.

I *do* know you.

But that can't be right.

No, maybe it was your mother.

His eyes were wider now
his arms flapping.

Or your grandmother perhaps.

You are the spitting image

of a girl I met

way back when.

Rebecca looked deep into his eyes
and a soft sad smile came over her face.

Of course, it can't be you

Seamus now said softly

but I'll never forget her

whoever she was.

Seamus Speaks

Declan, remember I told you about Katherine
the love of my life?
After she had left me
after she was dead
I was devastated.
I didn't want to live
not without her.
So I hitchhiked north
to Mullaghmore and walked out to the point.
The waves were more fierce than I'd ever seen
and it was an ugly
ugly day
a day fit for what I wanted to do.
I knew the currents there were deadly
and death was what I truly wanted.
I filled my coat pockets with heavy stones
and walked out on that ledge of those flat black rocks.
I would have ended my life then
happy to be rid of my pain
and what I saw to be a lonely miserable life ahead.

But then a girl came along
one who looked just like
like you, Rebecca.
She consoled me

and talked to me
and somehow eased the pain.
It was not a cure
but whatever she said
was enough to make me
toss those stones into the sea.
And she walked me back into town
and found me a ride home.
I never saw her again
until now.

Time to Leave

Well
Seamus said finally
                you look so much like her
                or at least the way I remember her.
                Again, I'm an old man
                with funny thoughts
                so forgive me.
And he bent over to collect the broken pieces
of the shattered teapot
and dropped them
into the garbage can.

RETURN TO STREEDAGH

Uncle Seamus became distracted and self-absorbed
after that.
And I said we had to leave.
I said he shouldn't worry about me
as he waved a hand in the air
and nodded that it would be okay.
He just wanted to be left alone
with his thoughts
for a while.

Rebecca seemed tired as we drove back to Streedagh
drifting off
but then coming back awake as we neared the shore.
        That was you at Mullaghmore
I said.

                Yes, I remember him.
                There were so many people
                I met over the years
                so much pain in their lives
                and I would try to help when I could.
                But all I could do
                was try.

A Fire of Peat

We drove over the little bridge
at Streedagh
and out onto the field with horses and sheep.
Here she pointed to a small cottage
among a cluster of other cottages.
            That's where I live
she said.

Inside it felt cold and damp
and she made a fire of kindling and peat
in the stone fireplace.
I looked at her arm
and the wound appeared to be healing already.
            It's not deep
she said.
And then I kissed her
and held her
and said
        I want to be with you
        and stay
        right here.
        I don't want this to ever end.

Never-Ending

We ate bread and cheese
and carrots she said she had grown herself
and drank from a bottle of wine.
And the word "love" was spoken
so many times
that it took on many meanings at once.

           Do you remember when
           I first made contact with you?
she asked.
      Yes.
           Do you remember when you
           could see me for the first time?
I nodded.
           It took a very long time to find you
           and to build the bridge
           but I needed you.
           And now that you are here
           I am sad
           because I feel that I've used you
           tricked you.
        It's not like that
I said.
        I came here
        to be with you.
        It was my decision.

It's you who is making me strong enough
to be able to go back.
I've been ashore here for far too long.
It's not the way things are meant to be.
But it's this connection to you
this love we feel for each other
that will make me strong enough
to go back to the sea.
And leave me?
Yes.

No!
Rebecca leaving me was the last thing
I wanted.
And now I had discovered
I was the one who would
send her back.
No
I said again, this time more softly.
Please.

Sad Days in Heaven

The next morning
we spoke no more
of the previous night's conversation.

                                        Instead
we began to live
                                    really live
as lovers
as husband and wife
as if
                                    we were not
from different worlds.
                                        As if
our life together
our time
                                    was infinite.
No talk of selkies.
No talk of either of us
                                    going back.
She knew my thoughts
but I could never fully know hers.
Instead   I read
her eyes
her touch.
I believed   I could read
her heart.

TIME

There are no clocks or watches or calendars for such days.
No mechanical calculation for such time
such living.
And as long
as I did not question
or plan for the future
or doubt who we were
it went on and on.

DRINK OF DARKNESS

And then one day
after a month had passed
(but that is just a guess)
I saw something in her eyes.
She grew sad without apparent reason
and I held her
hoping to never let her go.
And after a while
after I felt our hearts beating
blending into a synchronized rhythm
she pulled away
and went to the cupboard
drew out a small glass jar of a dark fluid.

        If you drink some of this
she said

        it will help you understand.

    What is it?

        It's made from plants found near the shore.

        It's a bit strong but necessary

        now that we are here.

    Here?

        This place where we have arrived.

I didn't know what she meant but decided not to ask.
I looked at the dark liquid.

        So maybe you are a witch after all

I said.

      No.

      Selkies are never witches.

      Trust me.

And of course I trusted her

as she poured a small amount of the liquid

onto my tongue

and I fell into a deep sleep.

Unfolding Story

I was drifting downward
into some dark chasm
but then
the darkness gave way to vision
and the story began to unfold:
I saw the fisherman first
the lonely fisherman.
And then his son.
I saw something in the sea
a sleek beautiful seal
moving toward the shore.
I noticed the eyes
deep and dark.

And then everything changed.
I was not looking at the scene
from the shore.
I was looking
at the shore.

I felt the pity
the deep compassion
she felt
for Liam.
It felt like I was drowning

at first.
But then everything changed
and I began to sense
the transformation
beginning.

It was a powerful
overwhelming
experience
unlike anything
I had ever known.
It was fueled by love
by need
and by
a deep inner force
that cannot
be put into words.

THE ARRIVAL

And then something changed again.
I was the observer again
watching as
Rebecca
swam ashore
and stood up
naked on the shoreline.
But I was not just an observer.
I was Liam
watching this unfold.
I felt his pain
his loneliness
transform
into impossible joy.

History

After that
there was another shift.
I was not seeing through Liam's eyes
but through my own.
I watched as
he took her hand
and walked with her
into his stone house
and time began to move forward.

I could see that Liam
was kind to her
and loved her
and she loved him back
and they were happy
sharing a simple life
by the sea.

And the story
much like the most vivid movie
I had ever seen
shifted forward in time
and I watched the fisherman age
and the little boy grow into a man
turn against her
leave.
And the man

the man she loved
grew old and then sick
and I watched him die
in his bed
with Rebecca there beside him.
I felt what she had felt
at the moment of his death
a loss so debilitating
that I wondered
that she too
did not die.
But she lived on.

And then I followed her
as she left the old stone hut
and moved from town to town.
I watched as Ireland changed around her.
But there was one constant:
people suffered losses
their hearts ached
and Rebecca absorbed their pain
tried to help
but often failed.
Many men fell in love with her
but she kept a barrier in place
around her emotions.
She moved on when
she knew she had to.

And I even saw the scene
saw every molecule of it
of a young Seamus on the rocks
at Mullaghmore
the giant waves pounding the shore
the stones in his pockets
the pain in his heart
and Rebecca walking up to him.

And then it grew quiet.
I saw Rebecca
living alone
first in a small cottage
at the foot of Knocknarea
and then beneath the shadow of Benbulben
and then there was a deep longing to be back
on the coast
and finally
I saw
Rebecca alone.
In this very cottage by the sea
where she would walk
almost daily to the ruins
of the stone hut
where I first met her.
And then I finally saw

                                        myself.

THE DREAMER AWAKES

When I awoke
the cottage was empty.
The peat fire had gone out
and the room was cold.
I was convinced I was still in
the drug-induced dream
the journey she had sent me on.
But now I could see that things
were different:
colours less vivid
everything less intense.
And I knew
I was back.

Emptiness swept over me
like a cold dark wave.
Rebecca was gone.
And all I felt next
was panic.

I went outside into the grey mist of morning
and began to run down the beach.
I ran until my lungs ached.
I screamed her name into
the rising sea wind.

When I couldn't run anymore
I stumbled on until I arrived
exhausted and without hope
at the remains of the stone hut
where I found her clothes
her dress and the scarf she had worn
and a note
a poem of sorts:

> Declan,
> Pain subsides
> love endures.
> Endings ensure beginnings.
> Memory survives.
> Remember me
> remember my voice
> and listen for it
> in the sea and in the wind
> and in your heart.
> > Love,
> > Rebecca

Return to Knocknarea

I asked Uncle Seamus to walk with me again to the top of Knocknarea. We picked a windless, cloudless day to find our way to the top and to the puzzling cairn, the tomb of Queen Maeve. I chose to not tell him anything more about my time with Rebecca. There was a haunting residual effect of the drug I had taken that made me doubt once again if I was fully capable of knowing what was real and what was imagined. It made me doubt myself and everything that had happened. Maybe the truth is what we believe it to be. I don't know.

From the top of the mountain, we looked west and north — out across to the expanse of sea in the distance and the beach of Streedagh somewhere out there.

More than ever I felt that I belonged to another time. I would leave Ireland and return home only because I knew it was the thing I had to do for my parents. I owed them that much because they were good parents, not ready to fully lose their son to a larger world. But they would probably never understand how I had changed.

Having lost Rebecca, I knew I must return home.

But it would be a temporary return. Rebecca had left me with sorrow but also the realization that there was a thread to everything that connected the past to the present and the future and that some of us had connections to places and people that ran much deeper than we could ever imagine.

And I'm sure Uncle Seamus was wondering what was going through my head as I stood there on the mountaintop staring off into the distance. Some things, he began to say. Some things, Declan … but his voice trailed off.

And then the sky grew dark and a big storm cloud blew in from the Atlantic. The wind began to rise again as we started our trek back down the mountain.

I listened, really listened to the song of the rising wind rushing at us from the distant sea and was certain I heard something. It was a voice.

Her voice.

At first I couldn't make out what she was saying. It was not like before — this voice inside my head. There were no words I could recognize. And it was like singing but it was not singing. As I listened I began to realize I was feeling what was inside her heart.

There is no single word of my own that I could possibly attach to that emotion, but there was sadness and there was love and longing as well. Both beauty and pain, and when I felt I could bear it no more, it faded.

When Uncle Seamus asked me why I was crying I couldn't begin to explain. So I said, "It's just the wind, Uncle Seamus. Just the wind."

By the time we were down the mountain I had begun to hear the voice clearly again, and it was most certainly her voice. There were words this time but I couldn't understand a single one. Yet that didn't trouble me. Perhaps it was ancient Irish Gaelic, maybe something else.

But I knew I would find a way to translate whatever language the wind was speaking. I yearned to learn it, to speak it, to make sense of all that had happened to me, and all that was yet to come.

LESLEY CHOYCE is the author of over ninety books of literary fiction, short stories, poetry, creative non-fiction, and young adult novels. He runs Pottersfield Press and has worked as editor with a wide range of Canadian authors. He has edited a number of literary anthologies and hosted several television shows over the years.

Choyce has taught creative writing at Dalhousie and other universities for over thirty years and has acted as mentor to many emerging writers. He has won the Dartmouth Book Award, the Atlantic Poetry Prize, and the Ann Connor Brimer Award. He has also been shortlisted for the Stephen Leacock Medal, the White Pine Award, the Hackmatack Award, the Canadian Science Fiction and Fantasy Award, and the Governor General's Award. He was a founding member of the 1990s Spoken Word rock band, The SurfPoets. He surfs year round in the North Atlantic.

www.lesleychoyce.com

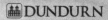